Julia
the Sleeping
Beauty Fairy

To Tabitha, Verity, and Thalia, from the fairies

Special thanks to Rachel Elliot

Text copyright © 2016 by Rainbow Magic Limited

ISBN 978-0-545-88737-3

10 9 8 7 6 5 4 3 2 1   16 17 18 19 20

Printed in the U.S.A.   40

First edition, January 2016

Julia
the Sleeping
Beauty Fairy

by Daisy Meadows

SCHOLASTIC INC.

Jack Frost's
Ice Castle

Forest

Tiptop Castle

The Fairy Tale Fairies are in for a shock!
Cinderella won't run at the strike of the clock.
No one can stop me—I've plotted and planned,
And I'll be the fairest one in all of the land.

It will take someone handsome and witty and clever
To stop storybook endings forever and ever.
But to see fairies suffer great trouble and strife,
Will make me live happily all of my life!

Contents

Over the Drawbridge

Rachel Walker rested her hand on the drawbridge chain of Tiptop Castle and looked down at the moat below. Her best friend, Kirsty Tate, was standing beside her, gazing at the green lawns and flower gardens that surrounded the castle. They had paused halfway across the drawbridge to admire the view.

"I feel like a princess standing here," said Kirsty in a dreamy voice. "It's just like something out of a fairy tale!"

"We're so lucky to be able to stay here for the Fairy Tale Festival," said Rachel, as the spring breeze ruffled her blond hair.

It was spring vacation, and Kirsty was staying with Rachel for a very special reason. Tiptop Castle was a beautiful old castle on the edge of Tippington, and this year it was hosting the famous Fairy Tale Festival.

"I can't wait to see all the people dressed up as fairies and fairy tale characters," said Kirsty.

"I wonder if we'll meet any *real* fairies," said Rachel.

The girls shared a happy smile. They

had been friends of the fairies ever since they met on Rainspell Island, and had shared many amazing adventures.

"Come on," Kirsty said. "Let's go inside."

The castle gatehouse was decorated with twinkling white lights. Inside was a festival organizer dressed as Puss-in-Boots. He waved his paw at Kirsty and Rachel, and then stroked his whiskers.

"Welcome to Tiptop Castle!" he said in a deep voice. "What are your names?"

The girls told him, and he checked them off on his list. Then he gave them a big smile.

"Please enter the castle and explore with the other children until lunchtime," he said. "You can go anywhere you like and look at everything. Have fun!"

"This is going to be amazing!" said Rachel, hurrying inside and gazing around the large entrance hall.

A chandelier hung from the ceiling, glittering with dangling crystals. More twinkling lights were wrapped around the banisters of a wide staircase, and suits of armor stood on each side.

"Where should we look first?" asked Kirsty.

"Let's go upstairs," said Rachel, taking her best friend's hand. "I want to see what a princess's bedroom looks like!"

The girls quickly ran up the staircase
and discovered a long, wide hallway. All
the doors were open, and they looked
inside each of them, gasping at what
they saw. Every room was decorated in
a different way. Rachel's favorite had
golden furniture and red velvet curtains.
The one Kirsty liked best had a silver
four-poster bed in the middle. It was
surrounded by white
drapes and topped
with a thick
canopy of
shiny satin.
Pretty blue
curtains
hung from
the tall
windows.

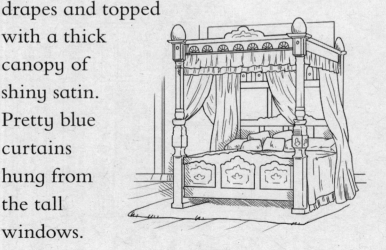

"It looks like a mermaid's bedroom," she said with a happy sigh. "Look— the mirror is decorated with tiny silver seashells!"

All of the bedrooms were so beautiful! When they reached the end of the hall they could hardly wait to see the rest of the castle. A second staircase led them back down to the ground floor, where they skidded across a polished oak floor into the music room.

"Look at the piano!" exclaimed Rachel.

A beautiful white grand piano stood on a blue rug. A huge mirror over the fireplace made the large room seem even bigger. Two big couches with clawed feet stood beside the fireplace. There were tall white lilies on every table.

"I wonder what's in there," said Kirsty.

She pointed to a set of double doors
that led into another room. When they
walked through, the girls discovered a
long dining room. A huge wooden
dining table sat in the middle. Silver
candle holders topped the table, and
paintings of kings and queens filled the
walls.

"This is just what I imagined a
fairy tale castle would be like," said
Rachel. "They must have amazing feasts
in this room!"

Just then, they heard the sound of
laughter outside the room.

"That must be some of the other kids
who are here for the festival," said
Kirsty. "Let's go and say hello."

She went to the door of the dining
room and stepped back out into the

hallway, but no one was there. Rachel joined her, and they heard footsteps running up the staircase.

"They must have gone to explore the bedrooms," said Rachel. "Never mind—I'm sure we'll meet them later. Let's see where this door leads."

She turned the handle of the nearest door, and they walked into a cozy reading room. Large, soft armchairs were arranged around the room next to polished side tables filled with snacks and jugs of water. The walls were lined with shelves of books that reached all the way to the high ceiling, and the girls gazed up at them in wonder.

"Look, there are ladders so you can reach the highest shelves," said Kirsty.

"Those reading chairs look really

comfy," said Rachel. "Let's choose some books and snuggle up in them."

She turned to the nearest shelf and gave a cry of surprise. One of the books was glowing! Feeling excited, Rachel pulled the book off the shelf and out fluttered Hannah the Happily Ever After Fairy!

Fairy Tale Lane

"Hello, Hannah!" exclaimed Rachel and Kirsty together.

"It's wonderful to see you both!" said Hannah, her eyes shining happily. "I've come because I know how much you like reading, so I have a surprise for you."

She waved her wand, and there was a tinkling sound as silver fairy dust sparkled around them. The girls shrank to fairy size and felt gauzy wings fluttering on their backs. Their eyes shone with excitement as they realized that Hannah was taking them to Fairyland.

In the blink of an eye, the reading room had disappeared. Rachel and Kirsty were standing on a narrow road lined with stone. There were seven pretty cottages spaced out along the road, with straw roofs, and roses and honeysuckle growing by the doors. The smoke that

came from the chimneys sparkled in
all the colors of the rainbow, and the
mouthwatering smell of freshly baked
cakes hung in the air.

"Welcome to Fairy Tale Lane," said
Hannah.

As she spoke, the cottage doors opened
and seven beautiful fairies peered out.
When they saw the girls, they came
hurrying over to say hello.

"These are the Fairy Tale Fairies," said Hannah with a beaming smile. "These four are Julia the Sleeping Beauty Fairy, Eleanor the Snow White Fairy, Faith the Cinderella Fairy, and Lacey the Little Mermaid Fairy."

"Hello," said Rachel and Kirsty.

"And these three are Rita the Frog Princess Fairy, Gwen the Beauty and the Beast Fairy, and Aisha the Princess and the Pea Fairy," Hannah finished.

"It's nice to meet you all," said Rachel,

smiling at the fairies. "I didn't know that there were Fairy Tale Fairies!"

"Oh yes," said Julia, whose auburn hair was tied in a loose bun. "Each of us takes care of a fairy tale and the characters in it."

"Without our care, the characters could get lost and the stories would be empty," added Eleanor.

Faith squeezed Kirsty's hand and smiled shyly.

"Hannah told us how much you like fairy tales," she said. "We have a present for you."

Lacey pulled a book from behind her back and handed it to the girls. It was so sparkly that it was hard to know whether it was gold or silver, and the title was written in swirly pink lettering:

The Fairies' Book of Fairy Tales

A silky pink
ribbon bookmark
dangled from the
pages.

"Oh, thank you!"
said Kirsty in a
thrilled voice. "It's
the most beautiful
book I've ever seen!"

Eagerly, Rachel opened the book
and turned to the first story. But to her
surprise, the page was completely blank.
She turned some more pages, and found
that they were all blank.

"I don't understand," said Julia, gazing
at the book in dismay.

She glanced over at her cottage
window, and then let out a cry of alarm.

"My magic jewelry box!" she exclaimed. "I always keep it on the windowsill, but it's not there!"

Exchanging worried looks, the other fairies dashed into their cottages. Seconds later they came back out, looking pale and anxious. All their magic objects had gone missing!

"This explains why *The Fairies' Book of Fairy Tales* is blank," said Julia with a groan. "But where could our magic objects be?"

"I can guess," said Kirsty suddenly.

She pointed to the end of the road, where some goblins were sneaking away! Each one of them had an object clutched in his hands.

"They've stolen the magic objects!" Rachel cried. "Come on, we can catch them if we're quick!"

The girls zoomed off through the air
as fast as their wings could flutter, but
before they could reach the goblins, Jack
Frost leaped out in front of them!

"Stop!" he snarled. "Those fairy objects
are mine now, and I'm taking them to
the human world!"

"No," said Kirsty, trying to sound brave. "They belong to the Fairy Tale Fairies. You should give them back."

"Tough luck," Jack Frost snapped. "I've had enough of silly fairies and princesses. From now on, all fairy tales are going to be about me, me, ME!"

The goblins had stopped at the end of the road, and they cheered when they heard what he said.

"Please stop!" cried Julia, flying up
to join the girls. "Just think of all the
children who won't have fairy tales
to read."

"I don't care," said Jack Frost with a
sneer. "And what's more, I'm going to
start with *Sleeping Beauty*. From now
on, it's going to be called *Sleeping Jack
Frost*!"

As the girls gave horrified gasps, there
was a loud boom of thunder. With a bolt
of icy magic, Jack Frost and the goblins
disappeared into the human world.

A Wooden Bed

Hannah and the Fairy Tale Fairies flew up to join Julia and the girls.

"Jack Frost has taken your magic objects to the human world," said Kirsty. "He's planning to make your fairy tales all about him, starting with *Sleeping Beauty*."

The fairies looked very upset.

"That means that the fairy tale characters must be in the human world, too," said Julia. "We have to get our magic objects back and return the characters to their stories, or fairy tales will be ruined forever."

"Please let us help you," said Rachel. "We can't let Jack Frost do this to our favorite stories!"

The Fairy Tale Fairies looked very grateful, and Hannah nodded.

"I think it would be a good idea to help Julia first," she said.

"Oh yes, please," said Julia. "I need my magic jewelry box to rescue Sleeping Beauty and return her to her story."

"Then we should go back to the human world right away and start looking," said Kirsty.

Julia nodded and, with a wave of her wand, she whisked all three of them back to Tiptop Castle. The girls found themselves standing in the cozy reading room, human-size again. Julia fluttered between them.

"Where should we start looking?" she asked in a breathless voice.

Before the girls could reply, they heard laughter coming from the big dining room next door.

"I wonder what's so funny," said Kirsty.

"Let's go and find out," Rachel suggested. "Julia, you can hide in my pocket if you want."

Julia slipped into Rachel's pocket, and then the girls ran through to the dining room. They found a crowd of giggling children wearing fairy tale costumes— from frog princes to enchanted princesses and fairy godmothers. They were all standing around the long dining table, and Rachel and Kirsty had to stand on tiptoes to see what they were laughing at.

A beautiful young woman was lying in

the middle of the table, fast asleep. She
was wearing a long golden gown with
huge puffed sleeves, and her raven-black
hair spread around her head in long,
silky coils. Her skin looked as smooth
as velvet.

"How on earth can she sleep through all this laughter?" Kirsty wondered aloud. "Who is she?"

"She's one of the festival organizers, of course," guessed a girl dressed as a pumpkin. "Why else would she be dressed like that?"

"It's strange that she's fallen asleep on the table," said Rachel.

"Maybe she's been working hard to get ready for the festival," Kirsty suggested. Then she lowered her voice. "Come on,

we have to start looking for Julia's magic jewelry box."

But as they moved toward the door, Julia peeked out of Rachel's pocket and then let out a squeak of surprise.

"That's not a festival organizer," whispered the little fairy. "That's Sleeping Beauty!"

Rachel and Kirsty stared at the princess, hardly able to believe that they were looking at the real Sleeping Beauty. Then Kirsty noticed something that made her heart thump. Four pairs of large, green feet were poking out from under the dining table!

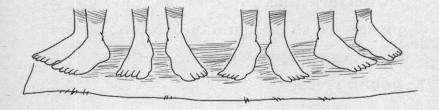

"Look!" Kirsty whispered, nudging Rachel. "Do those look like goblin feet to you?"

"Definitely," said Rachel with a frown. "Come on, let's get closer."

None of the other children had noticed the feet—they were all too busy giggling at Sleeping Beauty. Rachel and Kirsty crouched down beside the table and listened.

"My arms are aching from carrying that girl," complained a scratchy voice.

"Mine, too," said a deeper voice. "I don't see why we had to carry her all the way down from the big bedroom."

"Because Jack Frost needed the four-poster bed so he could be Sleeping Jack Frost, of course," squawked a third goblin voice.

"Speaking of Jack Frost, shouldn't we get back upstairs?" said a fourth goblin, sounding nervous. "He might want something and he'll be angry if we're not there."

"They're coming out," whispered Kirsty.

There was a scratching sound under the table, and then the girls saw the four goblins crawling out from under the table on their stomachs. They scrambled across the floor, unseen by the other children, and slipped out of the dining room.

"Quick, let's follow them," said Rachel. "They can lead us to Jack Frost!"

Grumbling Goblins

Kirsty and Rachel hurried out of the dining room and bumped right into the man dressed as Puss-in-Boots, who had met them at the entrance.

"Hi, Rachel and Kirsty," he said. "Are you having fun exploring?"

The girls groaned inwardly as the goblins disappeared up the stairs.

"It's been really exciting so far," said Rachel. "We were just going to have another look upstairs."

"That's fine," said Puss-in-Boots. "But remember, we'll be serving lunch in the garden, so don't miss it!"

He walked on, and Rachel and Kirsty ran up the stairs. The landing was empty.

"They've gone into a bedroom," said Kirsty. "But which one?"

Then they heard footsteps on the stairs behind them. They turned around and

saw a handsome young man dressed as
a prince coming toward them. He wore a
large felt hat with a
feather in it, and
his red tunic was
stitched with
gold thread.

"Good
morning," he
said, pulling
off his hat and
sweeping a low
bow. "I am Prince
Humphrey."

Rachel and Kirsty smiled at him,
guessing that he was another festival
organizer.

"We already know about the lunch
outside," said Rachel.

"Lunch outside?" repeated Prince Humphrey in a puzzled voice. "I don't know what you mean. I'm looking for Sleeping Beauty."

"That's the real prince from the fairy tale!" whispered Julia from Rachel's pocket.

"Oh my goodness, you've come to wake her up with a kiss, haven't you?" asked Kirsty in excitement. "She's downstairs in the dining room."

The prince darted back down the stairs, and the girls shared a smile before they hurried across the landing toward the bedrooms.

"Wait!" said Julia suddenly. "It will be easier to hide from Jack Frost if you are fairies, too. Can you find a place to hide so that I can transform you?"

There was a large statue of a fairy on the landing, and Rachel pulled Kirsty behind it. Then Julia flew out of Rachel's pocket and waved her wand. Instantly, the girls were fluttering their beautiful wings and hovering beside Julia. They made sure that no one was coming and then zoomed toward the bedrooms.

"The goblins mentioned a four-poster bed," said Rachel. "So Jack Frost must be in the silver-and-blue room that you liked best, Kirsty."

The three fairies flew to the open door of the bedroom and looked in. Jack Frost was lying on the beautiful silver bed, wearing a long blue nightgown and an old-fashioned nightcap. His head was buried in a plump pillow, and Rachel

noticed that his wand was lying on the ornate bedside table. The four goblins were lying on the floor around the bed, fidgeting and kicking each other. Each of them had a thin pillow, but they didn't look very sleepy.

"Get your foot out of my mouth!" squawked one.

"I can't help it! I can't get comfortable," said another.

Suddenly, Jack Frost sat bolt upright as if there were a spring inside him.

"You all are too noisy!" he roared at the four goblins. "How am I supposed to sleep with all this racket? BE QUIET!"

He flopped back onto the bed as the goblins froze with fear. Julia fluttered into the room and waved to Rachel and Kirsty, who followed her. They all perched on top of the satin bed canopy.

"My pillow's too bumpy," muttered one of the goblins.

"Mine's too squishy," said another.

"I'll take it," said a third, grabbing for the pillow.

Rachel, Kirsty, and Julia lay on their stomachs and looked over the canopy.

"Any sign of my magic jewelry box?" whispered Julia.

The girls shook their heads. All they could see was the tassel on Jack Frost's nightcap, and the squirming green limbs of the four goblins.

"It's no use," said Jack Frost. "I can't sleep."

"We can't sleep, either," wailed the goblins.

"Then you might as well give me your pillows," said Jack Frost. "Hand them over NOW!"

"It's not fair!" wailed the goblins as Jack Frost snatched their pillows. "You've already taken our blankets."

"I don't care about fair!" Jack Frost bellowed. "I care about ME! Now, sing me a lullaby."

"Oh no." Rachel groaned. She had heard the goblins sing before. "We might need earplugs."

Jack Frost sank back into the mound of pillows and the goblins linked arms and started to sing.

"Rock-a-bye Jack Frost on the soft bed.
When he shouts loud, it fills us with dread.
When he gets mad, the snowflakes will fall.
He'll keep our blankets, pillows and all."

Their squawky
voice made the
fairies wince. Jack
Frost pulled his
nightcap down over his
ears and plumped up his pillow.

"You call that a lullaby?" he snarled.
"Just be quiet and lie down."

"Look!" Kirsty hissed.

As Jack Frost plumped up his pillow,
he revealed the corner of an engraved
wooden box hidden underneath it. Julia
sharply drew in her breath.

"That's my magic jewelry box!" she
exclaimed. "Thank goodness we've
found it! But how can we get it back?"

Pillow Fight!

The goblins lay down again, grumbling under their breaths. Quietly, they pulled new pillows from under the bed. The fairies could only catch a few muttered words.

"The floors are too hard."

"It's so chilly!"

An idea suddenly popped into Rachel's head, and she turned to Kirsty and Julia with excitement in her eyes.

"Everyone loves a pillow fight," she
whispered. "We just need a few more
pillows . . ."

Julia laughed and flicked her wand. At
once, a huge mound
of soft pillows
appeared beside
the goblins,
who cheered
and flung
themselves
into the pile.
The fairies
zoomed down
from the canopy
and Julia returned Kirsty and Rachel to
their human form. Rachel picked up a
pillow and gently threw it at the nearest
goblin. He turned and glared at her for a

moment, then a huge, toothy smile
spread across his face.

"PILLOW FIGHT!" he yelled.

Seconds later, pillows were flying
through the air as fast as the goblins
could hurl them. They were throwing
them at each other as well as at the girls,
and Jack Frost started jumping up and
down on the bed in a rage.

"Stop it!" he shrieked. "I'm trying to
sleep!"

The girls couldn't help giggling as they flung pillows back at the goblins. Julia flew back to the canopy and used her wand to make more and more pillows, until the floor was completely hidden underneath them.

Feeling brave, Rachel took aim and hurled a pillow at Jack Frost's head. His nightcap came off and he shook his fist at her.

"We have to make him join in the fight and get him away from the magic jewelry box," Rachel said.

Kirsty grabbed another pillow and flung it at Jack Frost with all her might. He fell over backward and then bounced up again, red with anger.

"You pesky humans!" he screeched.
"I'll make you sorry for disturbing me!"

He snatched up his plump pillow and
threw it at them as hard as he could,
revealing the magic jewelry box lying on
the mattress. The girls ducked the pillow
and Rachel dived toward the bed. But
Jack Frost was too quick for her. With
a sneering laugh he snatched up the
jewelry box, jumped down from the bed,
and sprinted out of the room.

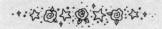

"After him!" Julia cried. "We can't let him get away again!"

Rachel and Kirsty raced after Jack Frost, who had pulled his nightgown up over his knees so that he could run faster. Behind them, they could hear the patter of goblin feet. Julia zoomed above their heads.

"He's going downstairs!" she called. "Faster!"

The girls ran downstairs and chased Jack Frost into the dining room. He skidded around the huge table and stood in the far corner, panting. The girls stopped to catch their breath, too, and then noticed that Sleeping Beauty was no longer lying on the table. She was sitting up, and her eyes were open. She was awake! Prince Humphrey was standing

beside the table and holding her hand.
They both looked at Jack Frost and the
girls in surprise.

"Where are the other kids?" asked
Rachel, looking around.

"They went outside to have some
lunch," said Prince Humphrey.

Sleeping Beauty blinked a few times
and then spoke in a soft, musical voice.

"I'm a little confused," she said.
"Where is my palace? Shouldn't I be in
my bed?"

"It's all Jack Frost's fault," said Kirsty,
looking at the goblin. "He stole Julia's
magic jewelry box. Without it, you can't
get back into your own story! We've
been trying to get it from him."

"In that case,
please allow us
to help you,"
said Sleeping
Beauty.

She jumped
down from
the table,
and Prince
Humphrey turned
to face Jack Frost.

"You'll never catch me," said Jack Frost, curling his lip. "A couple of little girls and two silly fairy tale characters are no match for the great Jack Frost!"

"We'll see about that," said Sleeping Beauty in a commanding voice. "I am a princess, and I insist that you give me that jewelry box right now!"

The Magic Jewelry Box

Prince Humphrey ran toward Jack Frost, who darted around the table in the opposite direction. Sleeping Beauty blocked his way, and he dodged sideways, diving under the table and scrambling out near the door. But Rachel and Kirsty were there, and he was forced to duck back under the

table again. Sleeping Beauty, Prince Humphrey, and the girls each crouched down at one side of the table.

"There's no way out," said Rachel, remembering what she had noticed in the bedroom. "Your wand is upstairs where you left it, so you can't escape by magic. Give us the jewelry box and we will let you go."

Just then, they heard the heavy patter of bare feet behind them, and the four goblins appeared in the doorway.

"Just in the nick of time," yelled Jack Frost. "CATCH!"

He tossed the magic jewelry box over Kirsty's head toward the door. But Kirsty sprang into the air, reaching her hands high above her head.

"Noooo!" shrieked Jack Frost as

Kirsty's hands closed around the box.

"Yes!" Rachel cheered in delight. "You didn't know that Kirsty's the best volleyball player in her school!"

Smiling with relief, Kirsty handed the magic jewelry box to Julia, and it immediately shrank to fairy size. Jack Frost jumped up in fury and banged his head on the underside of the table. A large lump appeared under his spiky hair.

"You annoying humans!" he snapped, clutching his head and crawling out from under the table. "Just you wait until I've got my wand in my hand!"

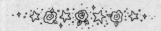

"It's too late," said Rachel. "Julia has her magic jewelry box back."

Jack Frost stuck out his tongue at her and then stomped out of the room with the goblins.

"Thank you both for all your help," said Julia, holding her magic jewelry box close to her heart. "I'll never forget your kindness— or your courage!"

She blew them each a kiss and then disappeared back to Fairyland in a shimmering haze of fairy dust.

Prince Humphrey clasped Sleeping
Beauty in his arms as they started to
shimmer and fade.

"Good-bye!" Sleeping Beauty called.
"Thank you!"

Moments later they had gone and the
girls were alone in the
dining room.

"Do you think
they've returned
to their story?"
asked Kirsty.

"I hope so,"
said Rachel as
her stomach gave
a loud rumble. "But
right now, I think we
should go and get some lunch with the
others!"

That night, Rachel and Kirsty felt like princesses as they got ready for their first night at Tiptop Castle. Their bedroom was at the top of one of the tall castle towers, and the tiny arched windows looked out over the glassy lake and the beautiful moonlit gardens.

"This is the most incredible room I've ever slept in," said Kirsty.

She gazed around at the dark wooden furniture, which had been polished until it gleamed, and the single four-poster beds with their drapes and canopies. Rachel flopped down on her bed and yawned, snuggling back against her feathery pillow.

"It's been a wonderful day," she said. "Oh, what's this? There's something hard under my pillow . . ."

She reached her hand under her pillow and drew out the sparkling book that the fairies had given them—*The Fairies' Book of Fairy Tales*.

Kirsty gasped in delight.

"I'd forgotten about our present in all the excitement," she said. "I wonder how it got there?"

"Magic," said Rachel with a grin.

Kirsty joined Rachel on her bed, and with their fingers crossed they opened the book and turned to the first story. They were relieved to see the words *Sleeping Beauty* at the top of the page. The story was in the book

again, and Sleeping Beauty and her
prince were both back where they
belonged.

"Let's read it before bed," Rachel
suggested.

The girls loved the story and had read
it together often. But this time, when
they read about the party that the king
and queen threw to celebrate Sleeping
Beauty being born, they discovered
something new. Kirsty leaned closer to
the picture.

"Look," she said in an awed tone. "Look at Sleeping Beauty's seven fairy godmothers."

Rachel leaned closer, too, and then shared a thrilled smile with her best friend. The fairy godmothers were the Fairy Tale Fairies!

When they reached "happily ever after," Rachel couldn't resist turning the page to see if the next story had reappeared, too.

"It's blank," she said with a sigh. "The other stories are still missing, and we have six more Fairy Tale Fairies to help."

Kirsty put her arm around Rachel's shoulders and smiled at her.

"Don't worry," she said. "As long as best friends like us stick together, I know that we can make a happy ending!"

THE FAIRY TALE FAIRIES

Rachel and Kirsty found
Julia's missing magic object.
Now it's time for them to help

Eleanor
the Snow White Fairy!

Join their next adventure in this
special sneak peek . . .

A Surprise Reflection

When Kirsty Tate opened her eyes, for a moment she couldn't remember where she was. She gazed up at the canopy that hung over her four-poster bed. A spring breeze had pushed open the gauzy curtains, and the sun lit up the white dressing table with its gold and silver swirls. On the dressing table lay a book with a sparkling cover—*The Fairies' Book of Fairy Tales*.

"Rachel, wake up," she said in a gentle voice. "It's our second day at Tiptop Castle!"

Rachel opened her eyes and gave Kirsty a sleepy smile. They were staying in a beautiful old castle on the outskirts of Tippington, where the Fairy Tale Festival was being held. Their bedroom was at the top of a tower of the castle, and the girls had agreed that it was fit for a princess—or two!

"What are you going to wear today?" asked Kirsty, hopping out of bed and opening the big wardrobe where they had hung their clothes.

"How about our fairy dresses?"

suggested Rachel, swinging her legs out of bed. "It will be fun to join in with everyone else."

The day before, all the festival organizers had been wearing fairy tale costumes. Kirsty clapped her hands together.

"That's a great idea," she said, "especially after our Fairyland visit yesterday!"

"I'm so happy that we managed to help Julia the Sleeping Beauty Fairy get her magic jewelry box back," said Rachel.

"And Sleeping Beauty and her prince are back in their story," Kirsty added. "But we have to do the same for the other fairies. They need their objects to look after their fairy tales."

She smiled as Rachel pulled on her mini backpack with its glittery fairy wings. It was funny to wear fake wings because they knew how it felt to have real ones!

RAINBOW magic™

Which Magical Fairies Have You Met?

- ☐ The Rainbow Fairies
- ☐ The Weather Fairies
- ☐ The Jewel Fairies
- ☐ The Pet Fairies
- ☐ The Dance Fairies
- ☐ The Music Fairies
- ☐ The Sports Fairies
- ☐ The Party Fairies
- ☐ The Ocean Fairies
- ☐ The Night Fairies
- ☐ The Magical Animal Fairies
- ☐ The Princess Fairies
- ☐ The Superstar Fairies
- ☐ The Fashion Fairies
- ☐ The Sugar & Spice Fairies
- ☐ The Earth Fairies
- ☐ The Magical Crafts Fairies
- ☐ The Baby Animal Rescue Fairies

■ SCHOLASTIC

Find all of your favorite fairy friends at
scholastic.com/rainbowmagic

HiT entertainment

RMFAIRY12

RAINBOW magic™

Magical fun for everyone!
Learn fairy secrets, send
friendship notes, and more!

■SCHOLASTIC

HiT entertainment

www.scholastic.com/rainbowmagic

RMACTIV4